THE LOST PENGUIN

AN OLIVER & PATCH STORY

FOR LIZ,
MY SECRET SIS
-CF

FOR WILLIAM
AND TILLY -KH

SIMON & SCHUSTER
First published in Great Britain in 2018 by Simon and Schuster UK Ltd, 1st Floor, 222 Gray's Inn Road, London WC1X 8HB • A CBS Company • Text copyright © 2018 Claire Freedman
Illustrations copyright © 2018 Kate Hindley • The right of Claire Freedman and Kate Hindley to be identified as the author and illustrator of this work has been asserted by them in
accordance with the Copyright, Designs and Patents Act, 1988 • All rights reserved, including the right of reproduction in whole or in part in any form • A CIP catalogue record for this
book is available from the British Library upon request • 978-1-4711-1733-6 (HB) • 978-1-4711-1734-3 (PB) • 978-1-4711-6869-7 (eBook) • Printed in China • 10 9 8 7 6 5 4 3 2 1

THE LOST PENGUIN

AN OLIVER & PATCH STORY

CLAIRE FREEDMAN AND
KATE HINDLEY

SIMON & SCHUSTER
London New York Sydney Toronto New Delhi

Oliver, Ruby and Patch were very best friends.
They did everything together.

Swinging high on the park swings.

Playing explorers.

Feeding the birds and . . .

. . . slurping vanilla-strawberry-mint specials in their favourite ice-cream parlour.

SPECIALS
• Mango
• Tutti frutti
• Coconut
• Gravy
PAMPERED POOCHES
DINE HALF-PRICE!

Best of all, they loved to visit the city zoo together.

'I love the lion! GRRRR!'
said Oliver, laughing.

'The meerkats are SO cute!' Ruby smiled.

But Patch had noticed a little penguin. He looked very sad.

PENGUINS "EUDYPTULA MINOR"
FROM: Australia New Zealand
LIKES: clupeidae cephalopods crustaceans

'Ah, you've found Peep,' said Sandy, the zookeeper.
'He's a rescue penguin. He's only just been brought here.'

'He must miss his old home,' said Oliver.

'He must miss his old friends too.
But I'm sure he'll settle in soon,' said Ruby.

And they waved to the little penguin
and set off for home.

PENGUINS "EUDYPTULA MINOR"

FROM: Australia
New Zealand
LIKES: clupeidae
cephalopods
crustaceans

The next day Oliver, Ruby and Patch visited the zoo again.
They went straight to see Peep.

But he wasn't there!

They ran to find Sandy to let her know.

'Oh no! Peep must have slipped out when I fed the penguins!' Sandy said.

'Maybe he's trying to get home,' said Ruby. 'But Peep's home is far away,' gasped Oliver.

'We'd better help you look for him, Sandy!'

TORTOISE POLISH
FINEST QUALITY

They looked everywhere they could think of in the zoo. Nothing.

So they tried the fountain.

No luck.

The fish shop.

Not a sniff!

Finally they walked slowly along the canal.

'Only ducks here,' sighed Ruby.
'It's getting late. What are we doing to do?'

THE MUCKY DUCK

Just then Patch started to bark excitedly,
his tail wagging round and round.

'PEEP!' cried Oliver
and Ruby together.

'It's all right, Peep!' said Ruby, gently stroking the frightened little fluffball of feathers.

They carefully carried Peep back to the zoo . . .

CLOSED

. . . but the gates were locked.

'We can take Peep back to my house,' said Oliver.
'But Peep is Patch's friend,' said Ruby.
'I think he should stay with us.'

'Why can't I have Peep?' said Oliver. 'You always have Patch!'
'But Patch is MY dog!' Ruby replied, rather unkindly.

They argued and argued.

'Fine!' yelled Oliver at last. 'You take Peep then!'
And he stomped off.

'OLIVER!' Ruby called tearfully. 'OLIVER! Please come back! Patch and Peep have GONE!'

'It's all my fault,' said Oliver. 'My shouting must have frightened them away.'

'Maybe Patch has taken Peep home,' said Ruby.

They raced to her house.

No Patch.

No Peep.

So they rushed to
Oliver's flat.

Nothing.

The only thing to do
was wait till morning.
They sat up very late
worrying and wondering.

It was a long night.

Next morning, Oliver woke very early.

'Ruby, if Patch and Peep aren't at my house
and they aren't at your house,

maybe they're at . . .'

'The zoo!' cried Ruby.

They arrived just as the gates were opening for the day.
Sandy was waiting for them.
'I knew you'd come,' she said. 'Look who's here.'

'Clever Patch!' said Ruby proudly.
'Woof!' barked Patch, sleepily opening one eye.

But when the time came to take Peep back
to his enclosure he began to look scared.

Then suddenly he was surrounded by a flurry of friendly
flapping penguins, all happy to welcome him back.

'See?' said Ruby, linking arms with Oliver.
'Home is where your best friends are.

Now, who's for a strawberry-vanilla-mint special?'